The Soft Open

Book One of the Ember & Wax Series

by Phoenix Cole

Where fire meets rhythm and every story is lit with song

Published by **Phoenix Cole Press**

The Soft Open

Book One of the *Ember & Wax* Series

Published by Phoenix Cole Press.

Phoenix Cole Press
Lewes, Delaware
www.PhoenixColeAuthor.com

This is a work of fiction. Names, characters, places, and incidents are products of the author's imagination or are used fictitiously. Any resemblance to actual persons, living or dead, events, or locales is entirely coincidental.

Paperback ISBN: 978-1-970946-01-7
Digital ISBN: 978-1-970946-00-0

Cover Design: Phoenix Cole Press Design Studio

Edited by: Ember Edit Suite · Compiled by Sentinel

Published in the United States of America

First printing, 2026

TABLE OF CONTENTS

Dedication

*For those who have ever lived in the shadows of their own truth
—
who have loved quietly, hidden pieces of themselves to survive,
and wondered if freedom was meant for someone else.*

*This book is for you — the hearts caught between two worlds,
learning to loosen your grip, to let the light in,
to finally breathe without apology.*

*And for those who have already stepped into the sun,
who live and love openly and lift others as they rise —
thank you for proving that liberation is possible,
and that love, once set free, is unstoppable.*

This is for the hearts that ache in silence—

for the ones who loved without permission

until they remembered they never needed it.

~Phoenix Cole

Before the Fire Had a Name

Before she built a sanctuary, Marina built a shell—a careful, invisible barrier that kept the world at bay.

It began quietly, almost imperceptibly: the pens aligned at right angles, the hospital corners on her bed, and the silent ritual of syncing her breath to the slow, unrelenting tick of a metronome. Small controls. Private victories. The world beyond her door was unpredictable, hungry, sharp-edged—but within the four walls she ordered with reverence, as if arranging scripture, she summoned stillness, building a shell to keep chaos at bay.

Her mother called it discipline.
Her father called it excellence.
No one ever called it fear.
But fear was the architect.

By twenty-five, Marina had become a master of disappearances. She knew how to be seen without being looked at. Her life was the color of bone—pale and stripped to essentials, clean, controlled, precise. She wore politeness like armor, turned herself into a woman who made others comfortable. Her reputation was unmarred. Her boundaries, unspoken but absolute. She knew how to perform proximity without risking intimacy.

It worked. But it hollowed her.

There was once a woman who ruined the illusion. Her name flickers now, half-buried in Marina's memory, like handwriting left in the rain. They met in a gallery on the East Side—she with ink on her fingertips, a laugh that didn't ask permission, a pulse that didn't dim in public. She moved through the world like music: uneven, alive, unashamed. And Marina, for a moment, followed the sound.

A brush of knuckles.
A pause too long between glances.

It ended as unsanctioned things often do: quietly, without witnesses. No scenes. No confessions. Just a subtraction, a vacancy where something might have been. Marina let it vanish without protest. She filed it away under things not meant to last, told herself nothing real had been lost if it had never been named.

But it stayed with her. Not the woman—Marina never let herself want someone long enough to mourn them—but the ache. The ache of almost.

Years later, passing an empty building with fractured windows and a silence she could shape, she felt the old ache swell. Not with longing, but with resolve. She didn't want to own a bar.

She wanted to build something.

A refuge. A place where longing didn't have to dress itself in apology. Where light wasn't something to avoid, but to bend—into warmth, into invitation. She would shape the sound. She would choose the scent. She would curate the rules and then unmake them. Here, control would become something else entirely. Not armor. Not hiding.

She called it ***Ember & Wax***—because every fire needs something soft to surrender to.

It became her altar. And in its low-lit glow, she rebuilt a version of herself that could pass for whole: polished, self-possessed, untouchable. Each evening, before the doors opened and the music bloomed, she stood in the threshold, hands pressed to the frame, breathing in citrus and smoke like absolution.

Some nights, when the speakers hummed and the lights danced across the floor, she would hear laughter echoing from a gallery that no longer exists.

And still, she doesn't turn around.

Because control—her oldest language—is still her sharpest prayer.

And inside these walls, she'd learn how to speak it with mercy.

CHAPTER ONE: OPENING IMAGE

PART I – THE FINAL CHECKLIST

The stemware was wrong.

A small thing—imperceptible to most—but Marina saw it instantly, and her jaw tightened on instinct. She plucked the highball glass from the bar tray with surgical precision, her movements smooth and unyielding, like a scalpel across silk. The crystal caught the overhead light and refracted it like a flaw begging to be magnified.

"James," she called, not bothering to turn. Her voice slid across the room with cool authority. "These are the old ones. The new glassware—etched crystal. Imported. Where is it?"

James appeared beside her, breathless and already folding under pressure, clipboard drooping like a dying orchid in one hand.

"Shit, sorry, I—"

She cut in with a blade of a smile. "It's fine. Just fix it."

He nodded, tray vanishing like a magic trick, and she pivoted toward the room—her temple, her cathedral of control.

Ember & Wax was nearly ready.

The lounge gleamed like the inside of a secret: bronze fixtures, velvet seating in deep garnet and obsidian, shadows falling with mathematical precision. From the mezzanine, warm Edison bulbs spilled gold over everything below. And the air—God, the air—was laced with orange peel and sandalwood, their custom scent blend, designed to stir nostalgia and appetite without ever quite revealing why. She had spent months perfecting that detail. It lingered now like a memory.

This was her favorite part.
The hush before debut.
The final breath before strangers entered and tried to undo her.

She walked the perimeter slowly, heels a steady rhythm on polished charcoal concrete, the kind of rhythm you could measure blood pressure to. Lighting: flawless. Tables: geometrically precise. Bathrooms: fully stocked with discreet baskets of amenities. Staff: nervous, but sharp-eyed and rehearsed.

The illusion of effortlessness.

At the host stand, she checked the time—4:49 PM. Exactly seventy-one minutes until *Ember & Wax* unveiled itself to the city's glittering darlings: tastemakers, influencers, critics who smelled weakness through their camera lenses. Seventy-one minutes of silence before the smile became real.

"Marina!"
She turned.
Jules, her floor manager, was waving a seating chart like it might burst into flames.

"VIP MIX-UP!!" Jules called. "They're demanding to sit near the stage."

Marina glided toward her, smoothing her blazer along the way. The fabric, sleek navy crepe, hugged her just enough to whisper restraint. Every inch of her said: I'm in control.

"Of course they are," she said, voicing a calm exhale. "Let me see." She leaned over the chart, eyes scanning.

No one would guess the quiet roar beneath her skin—the itch at the collar, the flutter beneath her sternum.

She hadn't eaten since breakfast.

Not from nerves, but food made her stomach misbehave when she was on display.

And tonight—All eyes would be watching. She adjusted two tables, recalculated foot traffic, and made the decision without hesitation.

No time to unravel.
No room for breath.
She was always holding her breath.

PART II – FAMILY ON THE LINE

She'd just adjusted the final dimmer in the back hallway when her phone vibrated. Again.

She didn't need to check the screen. Only one person called three times in a row.

"Hey, Ma," she answered, infusing her voice with a practiced lightness. "Finally," her mother said, crisp and mildly disappointed. "You never answer anymore. Still at that bar?"
"It's a lounge," Marina replied automatically, her voice clipped silk. "There's a difference."
"A lounge?" her mother repeated, as if it were a foreign word she didn't plan on learning. "This is what you went to business school for?"

Marina stared at the stack of folded event menus, exhaling through her nose. "This is my experience. My business. My networking."

A pause, quiet but charged.
"You know," her mother continued, faux-casual, "Ryan's mother ran into me at the market. He's back in town. Doing something in tech now. Something real."

Marina pressed her thumb into the edge of the countertop until the pad of her thumb blanched. "Good for Ryan."
"He always asked about you. Such a patient boy."
"Ma..." Too sharp. She reeled it back. "We've talked about this."

Another pause. Longer.
"You're not getting any younger," her mother said, voice dropping like a stone. "A man like Ryan won't wait forever."

Marina closed her eyes. Behind her lids, the lounge flickered gold and dusky.
"I have to go," she said, each word clipped clean.

"I just want you to be happy."
She ended the call before the guilt could sink in.

PART III – THE MASK AND THE MIRROR

The bathroom was a rare pocket of silence. Muted jazz seeped through the vents as Marina leaned into the mirror, reapplying lipstick with slow precision. Brick red. Matte. A color that broadcasted competence and closed doors.
Nothing soft. Nothing yielding.

She thought of that night in college—the stairwell, the almost. The scent of rain in her hair and hands that nearly found her jaw before pulling away.

The lipstick top dropped into the sink as if it were a grenade. She was snapped back.

The woman in the mirror looked to part. High-necked silk blouse. Gold hoops. Hair in its place. Polished, measured.
But up close, the cracks showed.
The tension in her jaw, the micro-tremor beneath one eye. The kind of strain that only mirrors notice.

When had it become performance? This curated version of her?

She snapped the lipstick closed and adjusted her blazer, locking it all back in place. The scent of citrus and sandalwood pressed heavier here—cloying at the edges.

She turned off the light before she could look again.

PART IV – EMBER & WAX COMES ALIVE

By 6:10 PM, *Ember & Wax* was full.

The room buzzed with curated cool—muted clinks of craft cocktails, hushed laughter spilling from candlelit corners, and the quiet hum of exclusivity. Guests lounged in shadows designed to flatter, beneath lighting that warmed even the iciest of affectations.

Marina moved through them like choreography—graceful, composed, untouchable.

"Marina!"

She turned. Avery, one of the bartenders, grinned from behind a neat stack of coupe glasses. Black-on-black outfit, vintage brooch flashing like a secret.

"You look criminal tonight," they purred. "If I didn't know better, I'd say you were trying to seduce the whole damn room."

Marina smiled—polished, practiced. "I'm seducing their wallets."Avery leaned in, lips quirked. "And here I thought you didn't like attention."

"I like control," Marina replied, as she turned to go.

But Avery caught her wrist for just a second. Playful. Meaningful. Skin on skin.

"You should let someone else take the lead sometimes," they said, then vanished back into the gleam of the bar.

Marina stared after them longer than she meant to.

Her fingers still tingled. And she didn't know if she liked it or hated it.

PART V – THE EAVESDROPPED TRUTH

She was checking the lighting by the back bar when she heard it.

Two women—one in a structured blazer, the other with a buzzcut and lipstick like spilled merlot—stood with their backs to her. They didn't see her. They were in mid-conversation, voices low, and relaxed.

"I didn't come out for them," the buzzcut said. "I did it for me. I couldn't keep living like I was apologizing for existing."

The other nodded slowly. "Same. My mom cried for three days. But I finally felt like I could breathe."

8   Marina stilled.
She shouldn't be listening. But she couldn't move.

"I just don't think hiding is sustainable," one of them said, lifting her glass. "It's poison in slow motion." They both laughed, soft and knowing.

Marina did too—but hers didn't reach her eyes.
She turned before they could see what was written on her face. Reaching for a water glass, her fingers shook just enough to spill a trail of condensation down her wrist.

It felt too much like relief.
And she hated that.
Hated how good it felt to feel.

CHAPTER TWO: THEME STATED

PART I – THE WATCHFUL EYE

From the mezzanine, *Ember & Wax* looked like a dream spooled onto celluloid.

Below, everything shimmered—cocktails catching light in coupe glasses, silhouettes draped like poetry over velvet seating, laughter blooming and fading in waves, like improvised jazz. Marina observed her art in motion. She leaned against the railing, one hand curled around the polished wood, the other cradling a glass of rosé she barely drank.

From up here, the lounge looked perfect.
Distance preserved the illusion.

Below, guests moved freely, folding into each other without performance or self-consciousness. A woman in a backless silk dress threw her head back in laughter, fingertips resting lightly on the wrist of the woman beside her like it was the most natural gesture in the world.

Marina couldn't hear the punchline, but she could feel its freedom. She sipped the wine—warm, flat, forgotten.

Behind her, footsteps whispered across the wood.

PART II – JULES, UNFILTERED

Jules flopped beside her in a flare of a movement, fanning themselves with the cocktail list like it was a lifeline.

"They're already calling it the best new lounge on the east side," they said, eyes glittering with mischief. "Someone just described the lighting as 'filmic.' I can't tell if that's a compliment or a veiled insult."

Marina cracked a small smile. "Depends on the film."

Jules offered her their Negroni. Marina shook her head. Jules shrugged and took a long sip. "You should be proud," Jules said, scanning the crowd with the kind of ease Marina could never quite emulate. "You built this. And you're still standing. Miraculously!"

Marina exhaled through her nose. "Give it twenty minutes."

Jules nudged her. "You ever think about actually relaxing?"

"Can't risk it. What if someone uses the wrong coasters?"

A grin spread across Jules's face. They leaned in, voice lowered. "You always like this?"

"Obsessive? Anxious? Rigid beyond repair?" Marina asked.

"I was gonna say 'mysterious,' Jules said, grinning, "but sure. Let's go with those too."

Marina arched a brow. "You want to toast me or read me?"

"Why not both?" Jules rhythmically tapped their glass. "You're a riddle wrapped in a designer pantsuit."

The moment hovered, almost flirtatious, until Jules added, almost as an afterthought, "Reminds me of my ex. She wore polish like armor. Took years to peel it back."

Marina's hand steadied on the railing.
She smiled, lips tight, but said nothing.
Jules didn't notice. They were already slipping away. "Text me if the world ends."

The mezzanine felt colder once she was alone again.

PART III – THE LIE OF CURATED PERFECTION

Back in the office alcove behind the bar, Marina sat down for the first time in hours. The hum of the lounge was muted by thick glass, the world outside pressed into hush.

She unlocked her phone.
Ember & Wax had already been tagged in over fifty stories.
Angles like magazine spreads.
Cocktails glowing like jewels.
Captions dipped in clever seduction.

She scrolled:
"Vibe of the year."
"New favorite spot 😍"
"Aesthetic violence (in the best way)."
"Tastefully sensual atmosphere."

Every photo glowed. Every image drenched in gold and shadow. Every filter flattered.

She flipped to the selfie camera.

Her reflection stared back, composed and unyielding. Hair smoothed, lipstick fresh, blazer crisp. She snapped a photo—habit more than intention—and studied it.

This wasn't her.

But it was the only version she trusted the world to see.

She didn't post it. She just locked the screen and set the phone down, face-first.

PART IV – VOICES IN THE VELVET

She took the long way back through the lounge—needed to stretch her legs, clear her mind, find her pulse again.

Towards the rear, in the dimmest corner, two women nestled into a velvet loveseat. Their bodies leaned in, knees brushing. One of them—petite, expressive—told a story with animated hands. Her voice rose and dipped with the memory of a terrible date. The other woman laughed—a deep, unguarded laugh—and reached over, hand resting on her thigh.

"You're so bad," the first said, grinning.

"Only when it's worth it," came the reply as her lips curled into a wide, unapologetic smile.

They looked at each other with an ease Marina felt in her chest-like warmth uncorked.

They didn't glance around.

Didn't lower their voices.

They simply were.

Marina paused.

Not to eavesdrop.

But to study.

What would it feel like to laugh like that, unafraid? To touch and be touched without searching for witnesses?

She didn't envy their joy.

She envied their ease.

PART V – ONE SMALL SHIFT

The petite woman noticed her.

She looked up, smiled—gentle, open, uncomplicated—and nudged her partner's arm playfully.

The second woman followed her gaze.

Both looked at Marina.

And for once...

She didn't look away. She held the gaze just a beat longer than necessary, a breath longer than polite. Then she nodded, a soft acknowledgment, and turned toward the main bar.

Her heart beat hard—not from fear, but from something lighter.

Louder.

Not a declaration.
Not a coming out.
But something.

A quiet shift.
A private tremor.
The softest open.

CHAPTER THREE: SET-UP

PART I – UNWANTED GUESTS

Ryan showed up before dessert.

Marina had just stepped off the floor to confirm details with the valet when she spotted him near the door—polished shoes, too-white teeth, blazer priced more for ego than taste. His hands were buried in his pockets like he wanted to seem casual, like he hadn't carefully planned this entrance.

Of course, her mother had told him. And of course, she hadn't told Marina.

Marina didn't wave.
She waited.

He spotted her, lit up with a smile that struck arrogance, and crossed the room like a man who assumed welcome.

"Marina," he said. "Wow. This place is..."
He glanced around, blinking slowly like he was about to make something up.
"...cool."
"Thanks," she said, tight as thread. "We're busy tonight."
"Oh, no, totally," he said, already leaning in for a hug she did not return. "I just wanted to stop by. Your mom said you were doing something big, so I figured—why not show support?"

Marina bared her teeth in a smile.

"You're here because she sent you."

He blinked. Then grinned, trying too hard. "Well, you know her. She's proud. Still tells people you're the most eligible woman in the Tri-County area."

"Is that so," Marina said flatly.

Ryan glanced over at the bar. "Think I could grab a drink?"

"You're welcome to wait," she said. "Like everyone else."

He raised an eyebrow. "Wow. Okay."

She didn't wait for a response—just turned and walked off, spine rigid as a steel cable.

Avery had watched the exchange between Marina and Ryan, head tilting slightly as she caught the tail end of it. Most people wouldn't have noticed the subtle shift in Marina's posture, the clipped edge in her silence. But Avery did. Marina was furious.

As Marina passed on her way to the kitchen, Avery caught the faint purse of her lips and raised an eyebrow.

"You good?" They asked, voice low.

"Peachy," Marina muttered, not breaking stride.

PART II – THE DINNER TABLE (FLASHBACK)

Three nights earlier, her mother had made risotto, set the table for three, and one seat remained conspicuously empty.

"Ryan's back in town," she said, like announcing spring. "His startup's doing very well."

Marina sipped her wine instead of responding.

"He asked about you," her mother continued.
"Did he?," Marina replied.

Her mother put down her fork—delicately, deliberately. "You need someone who understands your world."
"I understand my world," Marina said.

Her mother gave a smile that didn't quite reach her eyes. "That's not the same as sharing it."

There was nothing left to say. And nothing that would have mattered.

PART III – CRACKS IN THE SURFACE

Later that night, after the guests had gone and the lighting had dimmed to its final flicker, Marina locked the front doors and stood in the quiet hush of the empty lounge beside Jules and Avery.

"You're quiet," Jules said.

Marina looked at them.

"Quieter than usual," Avery clarified, nudging gently.
"I'm fine," Marina said.
Then paused.
"Just... a long night."

Avery nodded once.
"He looked like a spreadsheet in a blazer."

Marina blinked, confused.
"Your ex," Avery said. "Ryan. That was him, right?"
She paused, then gave a small nod.
"God," Jules said. "Men named Ryan are either gay or terrible. Sometimes both."

Marina let out a sound—half laugh, half breath. Real. Unfiltered.
Jules smiled like it was a win.
They didn't ask more.
Didn't push.

No one mentioned the flicker in Marina's eyes when she thought no one was watching. The way her gaze lingered on couples who didn't hide. The way her hand hovered, just slightly, when someone brushed hers in passing.

They didn't say it.
But they saw her.
And for now...
That was enough.

CHAPTER FOUR: CATALYST / INCITING INCIDENT

PART I – UNSCHEDULED SOUNDCHECK

It was technically after hours, but the bass was already awake.

A low thrum vibrated through the floor of *Ember & Wax* like the building itself had a pulse—steady, alive, and aching to be felt.

Marina stepped inside, drawn by the sound, and found the lounge bathed in deep, smoldering red light. The stage glowed like coals, casting the entire space in the color of danger.

She paused.

At the riser, behind a new turntable setup, a woman stood in silhouette—headphones crooked over one ear, one hand adjusting a dial, the other lifting a drink. She was absorbed, nodding along to the rhythm, wholly at home.

Then she looked up.

And Marina froze.

The woman smiled.
Not politely.

Not professionally.

It was a smile that said: *I see you.*

PART II – FIRST CONTACT

She hopped down from the riser like gravity was optional. Cargo pants. Combat boots. Black tank. Confidence worn loose over her shoulders like a favorite hoodie. Her eyes were a rich, unreadable amber beneath thick brows. Hair messy and sculpted all at once—short at the sides, curls wild and deliberate on top.

"You must be the boss," she said, voice smooth, smoky. "Or you just dress like one."

Marina straightened. "Yes, I'm Marina. The owner."

"Thought so." The woman pulled off her headphones and extended a hand. "Logan."

Marina hesitated a second too long before shaking it. Logan's grip was warm, a little calloused. And neither of them let go right away.

Marina cleared her throat. "You're early."

Logan's mouth tilted in a grin. "You're welcome."

"You weren't scheduled to rehearse until tomorrow."

"Yeah, but tomorrow's boring," Logan said, glancing around like she already belonged. "Had a feeling this place would sound better at night."

Not arrogance—ease. Like the space had chosen her, not the other way around.

Marina fought the reflex to tuck a stray hair behind her ear. Instead, she folded her arms.

"I appreciate initiative. But I run a tight schedule."
Logan tilted her head. "Oh, I can tell. You've got clipboard energy."
"Clipboard energy?"
"Yeah," Logan said. "Like... dangerous clipboard energy."

Marina opened her mouth. Closed it. Something flickered in Logan's eyes—amusement, curiosity, maybe something more.

"Want to hear something?" Logan asked.
"I don't really have time—"
"Just stay for one," she said, already turning back toward the decks.

Before Marina could reply, the bass dropped.
Not loud. Not aggressive. Just low—like a secret spoken close. The rhythm slid into her bones before it reached her ears. Then came layers: synth, textured and slow; the hiss of vinyl crackle; a vocal loop—just a breath, just a sound—that wrapped around her like smoke laced with memory.

It wasn't the kind of music Marina usually noticed.

But she couldn't look away.

Couldn't move.

She stood still, arms crossed, tension blooming in her chest—and let it fill her.

PART III – AFTER THE DROP

The track faded.

Logan turned back slowly, eyes steady—already knowing what Marina was going to say, and clearly waiting to hear her say it anyway.

"Well?" Marina hesitated, her gaze flicking to Logan's mouth for a fraction too long. "It's... good."

Logan let out a low laugh, head dipping slightly before tilting —her eyes dragging back up to meet Marina's. A smirk tugged at her lips.

"Just good?"

Marina's mouth twitched—she tried not to smile, but it broke through anyway.

"I'm not easily impressed."

Logan stepped forward. Just one step. But the air changed—became charged.

"Mm. Noted. Neither am I." Logan's smile widened, slow and deliberate. "I'll try harder."

For a second, Marina's brain short-circuited.
She reached for professionalism like it was a lifeline.

"You'll have full access to the sound system for rehearsal tomorrow. We'll finalize your set schedule then."

Logan nodded, unfazed. "Looking forward to it. And to seeing how dangerous your clipboard really is."

Marina didn't answer. She turned sharply, heels clicking across the polished concrete—faster than necessary.

But even after the door closed behind her, the beat lingered.
It followed her like a second heartbeat.

CHAPTER FIVE: DEBATE

PART I – NOT HER TYPE

Marina didn't have a type.

At least, that's what she told herself.

Because admitting otherwise meant naming something she wasn't ready to want. It meant dragging desire out of the shadows and holding it up to the light.

But Logan wasn't hypothetical. She was here. In the flesh.
In the lounge. All swagger and sound.
All rhythm. All low, dangerous charm.
Marina thought, *What the hell?*

The next morning, she walked into the office telling herself it was just another day.

She opened the invoice folder, assigned the files, started her laptop. Her fingers hovered too long over the keyboard.

She opened two tabs—one for the spreadsheet, one for her email. Clicked between them, back and forth. Half-finished messages.

A spreadsheet she'd already formatted twice.

A third tab. Then a fourth.

She told herself she was focused.

She wasn't.

Logan had only been in the room for seven minutes. Maybe eight. But she had taken up permanent residence in Marina's mind, looping through memory like a favorite track on repeat.

PART II – GROUP TEXT, CHAOS EDITION

Marina's phone buzzed. It was from Jules.

Jules: *So, who is the DJ and why do I suddenly feel like a gay teen again?*

Marina could practically see Jules grinning, biting their lip in nostalgic amusement.

Avery: *Logan??? DEADLY. I would risk everything including my skincare routine.*

Marina laughed—quietly, in her normal subdued way—because she could see Avery's brows arched high, smirking like a queer cat with a secret.

Jules: *Did you see the forearms??*
Marina?
You okay??

Marina stared at the screen, thumb hovering. Thought about not replying. She didn't have time to unpack her own head, let alone invite commentary.

Still, she typed: *Professional boundaries exist for a reason.*
Avery: *So that's a yes?*

She set the phone down—face-first—like it might burn her if left exposed too long.

PART III – MIRROR QUESTIONS

That night, Marina stood in front of her bedroom mirror.
Face clean.
Hair tied back.
Unarmored.
She stared at her reflection longer than necessary.

If she had been born into a different family—or grown up in a town where one could love openly—or if she'd had just one friend, at seventeen, who knew what it meant when you stared at your best friend for a second too long...

Would it have changed everything?
Would she be someone else?

Her fingers hovered near her lips. Her lips still remembered smiling—helplessly—when Logan had murmured, I'll try harder.

She scowled. Snapped off the light.

And walked away before her reflection could ask more questions.

PART IV – LATE NIGHT GHOSTING

The next day, her phone vibrated.

Logan: *Heard you like a tight schedule. What's the verdict on mine?*

Marina stared at the message.
Typed.
Deleted.
Typed again.
Deleted again.

Put the phone down.
Picked it back up.

Finally—
Marina: *Rehearsal confirmed. 9 PM slot.*

A pause.

Logan: *Oh. Okay. Just business? That's cold. Very clipboard.*

Marina: *It's professional.*

A beat.

Logan: *Fair... For now.*

Marina didn't respond.
She left the chat open, the screen glowing softly in her hand like something half-forbidden.
She set it aside again.

But her *heart?*
It didn't follow instructions.

CHAPTER SIX: FIRST CONNECTION

PART I – REHEARSAL HOUR

9:07 PM. Rehearsal Hour.

Marina rarely ran late.

She hated the feeling—like losing control one minute at a time
—but she'd spent the day inventing distractions: a "rescheduled"
food delivery, a staff walkout that never materialized. All to avoid
this exact moment.

And yet, she still arrived.

She stepped into the main lounge, and the space exhaled around
her. Empty, ***Ember & Wax*** felt almost alive—shadows pooled
beneath velvet seating, light hummed in the bulbs like secrets being
whispered.

Logan was already at the booth, headphones tipped off one ear,
coaxing a low thrum from the soundboard until it curled into the
room like smoke.

"You're late," Logan said, not looking up.

"Blame the tuna tartare," Marina replied, pulse betraying her.

Logan glanced up, amber eyes catching and keeping. Then, with a grin: "That's a new excuse."

Marina exhaled—slow, measured—and walked toward the riser.

"You brought paperwork to a soundcheck?" Logan teased, gesturing to the clipboard.

Marina blinked.

It was hers.

Logan must've grabbed it off the desk, she thought.
Then answered herself: Of course she did.

Marina should've taken it back.
She didn't.
Instead, she leaned in to skim the set notes beside her—close enough to catch the scent of clean cotton... and something deeper underneath. Logan's scent.

"I knew you'd appreciate the symbolism," Logan said, tapping the clipboard like it had teeth.

Marina scanned the paper. Neat handwriting. Intentional.
She hated how much that turned her on.

"Your transitions are tight," Marina said. "You plan for crowd flow?"

"I plan for bodies," Logan replied easily. "Where they'll gather. Where they'll breathe. Where they'll get braver."

The line landed in Marina's stomach like a pulse.

Logan turned back to the table, dropped a beat into the speakers, and adjusted the house lights with one hand. The lounge responded like skin to touch—shadows deepened, red melted to violet, edges softened to silk.

"Why music?" Marina asked before she could stop herself.

Logan looked over. "Why breathing?"

Then softer: "Because it tells the truth, even when we won't."

"You always this nosy?"

"You always this composed?"

Marina arched a brow and tilted her head. "I'm precise."

"And you're private," Logan said. "That's different."

It stopped Marina—just for a second. She turned toward the stage lights.

"That's presumptuous."

"That's accurate."

Marina folded her arms. "What do you think you've read?"

"That you spend a lot of time making sure no one can," Logan replied.

Silence.

Bass threaded the quiet like breath through tension.

Marina leaned back against the riser. Suddenly, standing took effort.

"What's your read on this place, then?"

Logan slid her a soda with lime—fingertip grazing hers in the pass. A light, testing touch.

Electric.

Logan looked around the lounge—at the textures, the layered lighting, the curated imperfection.

"It's beautiful," she said. "But like it's trying very hard not to be seen too clearly."

Marina said nothing, but her heart beat louder than the music.

Logan tilted her head. "What are you trying to do, Marina?"
Then, lower: "With this place. With you."
"Keep it from collapsing," Marina said.

The truth slipped out before she could smother it.
Logan watched her like the track had just shifted keys.

"That's survival. Not ambition."
Then quieter still: "You ever want something else?"

Marina didn't answer.
She just looked at her.

PART II – THE ALMOST

Silence wrapped thick around them.

Marina's head felt light—air thinning under the weight of unspoken things.

But she didn't speak.

She turned away, back to her checklist, her clipboard, her sanctuary.

Logan held her gaze a few beats longer, then returned to the turntables.

They started working in rhythm after that. Marina with logistics. Logan with loops. Music low and sultry—designed for proximity.

They hadn't moved much.
But somehow, they were closer now.
Shoulder to shoulder.
Breathing to the same measure.
In tune.

They glanced at each other at the same time.
The air shifted.
The temperature climbed.
The room warmed to a slow, steady burn.

Logan's eyes dropped—just once—to Marina's mouth.
Marina felt the heat rise along her neck like a confession.
Then Logan's voice, low and unhurried:
"If I kissed you right now…"

"...would you stop me?"

Marina's breath caught.

She didn't speak.

A beat passed.
Then another.
Then another.
And for once—Marina didn't lie.

"No."

Their eyes locked.
And held.

Then—

The kitchen door banged open.

Jules' voice cut through the moment like a blade. "We're out of ginger syrup—again!"

Spell broken.

Marina straightened so fast her spine ached.
Logan blinked.
The silence shattered like glass.

Marina cleared her throat. "I should—"
"Another time," Logan said, smile crooked, electric.

"Maybe," Marina replied.

But her voice sounded like yes.

"Yeah," Logan said, already turning back to her equipment. "Maybe."

But it hung between them.
Definite.
Undeniable.

Another time.

CHAPTER SEVEN: OBSTACLE INTRODUCED

PART I – UNINVITED AGAIN

Friday night.
The lounge was packed—air thick with citrus, conversation, and curated cool.

Marina moved through it like she always did—composed, calculating, never flinching. Adjusting seating. Checking headcount. Smoothing chaos like silk over friction.

Until she saw *him...*

RYAN!
At the bar.

AGAIN—

Same blazer.
Same smirk.
Same misplaced confidence.

He waved. Like this was cute. Like we were still close.
Her stomach sank.

She moved through the crowd with surgical grace, her heels sharp punctuation marks against the floor. She stopped just short of him.

"You're not on the list," she said.
Ryan raised his glass. "You sound like a bouncer."
"I'm serious."
He held up both hands, faux-charming. "Relax. I know the owner."
"No. You know my mother."

He leaned on the bar like he belonged there. "Look, I just thought... maybe we could talk."
"About what?"
"About us."
"There is no *US*," Marina said. Her voice was quiet steel.
"You haven't returned my texts."
"Was I supposed to? I've been busy."

He gestured around the lounge, palms up. "With this?"
Her eyes narrowed. "With everything."
Then—

His gaze flicked past her.
And something changed.
His smirk sharpened as he said, "Ohhh."

Marina turned—just in time to see Logan moving toward the DJ booth. Headphones in hand. Expression unreadable.
She didn't break stride.
Didn't stop.
But she saw.

And Marina knew it.

Logan played like she was rewriting gravity.

Every sound in **Ember *&* Wax** felt heavier that night—the baseline a pulse through the ribs, the lights shifting in time with heartbeats, the air thick with recognition. Logan stood behind the decks, movements surgical. Not cold. Just contained. Controlled.

Marina watched from the far end of the bar, one hand wrapped too tightly around her glass.

The set wasn't angry. It was exact. Meticulously precise.
Each transition landed with brutal grace, the kind that says, I know exactly what I'm doing—and who's listening.
And Marina was listening. Too much.

The music built. Swelled. Broke.
People danced, oblivious to the fact that every note felt like a boundary being redrawn.

Jules leaned beside Marina, voice just audible over the beat. "You look like you're watching a breakup in real time."
Marina didn't look away. "Maybe I am."
"Did you do something?"

Marina's jaw tightened. "Define something."
Jules' laugh was soft. "That's a yes."

The track shifted—bass dropping into something slow, breathless. Logan's head tilted, her profile catching the red light just so. For a second, Marina thought she was looking right at her.
Then the drop hit, and Logan's gaze flicked away.

PART II – AFTER THE SET

The crowd clapped, scattered cheers spilling over into laughter and chatter. The kind of noise that fills the silence when something more personal should've been said.

Marina didn't move.
Twenty minutes later, Marina found and cornered Logan.

"*Logan—*" she started.
Logan didn't stop packing. She packed her gear with careful precision. Every coil wrapped tight, every motion deliberate. Professional. Too professional.

When Marina finally approached, Logan didn't turn.

"Good set," Marina said.
"Thanks."
"I mean it."

Logan's shoulders rose in a breath that might've been a sigh. "You usually do."

Marina hesitated, glancing toward the tables—empty now except for staff wiping down glasses.

"Can we talk?"

Logan didn't stop packing. Bent over her gear bag, rifling through cables and adapters. "Busy. No time."

Marina reached out, touched her forearm—lightly, just enough.

"Please. Just wait—"

Logan finished coiling the last cable. "About?"

"Earlier. Tonight."

Logan froze for a fraction of a second—just enough to betray that she remembered every second.

Then she turned, face neutral. "There's nothing to talk about."

Marina's throat worked around words she couldn't form. "You don't have to pretend."

"I'm not pretending." Logan's tone stayed even, but her eyes weren't.

"Please, talk to me." Marina's tone was hurt and yearning.

"Boyfriend?" Logan's voice softened—gentle, not forgiving.

"No," Marina said, too quickly. "Ex. My mother's favorite delusion."

Logan arched an eyebrow. "You looked cozy."

"I'm not—he's not—God, this is just messy. Let me explain,"

"You don't owe me anything. And I don't owe you a scene."

That stung.

Marina swallowed hard. "I—"

"I know." Logan's smile flickered like a dying light. "That's the problem."

The space between them felt wider than the entire lounge.

Logan turned back to her setup, shoulders tight beneath the glow.

Marina stayed there, unsure which silence to break first—the one in the room or the one in her chest.

PART III – JULES' INTERVENTION

Jules found her still there fifteen minutes later.

"Okay," they said, plopping onto a barstool, "you're officially haunting your own establishment."

Marina blinked. "I'm fine."

"Liar."

"I said something stupid."

"Just one?" Jules teased lightly. "You're improving."

Marina didn't smile. "She thinks I'm playing games."

Jules sipped their drink, watching her. "Are you?"

"No."

"Then tell her."

"It's not that simple."

"Marina," Jules said softly, "you're the queen of complex excuses. But sometimes 'I'm sorry' is the only real sentence left."

Marina stared down at her drink. "I don't think she'd believe it."

"Then don't say it," Jules said. "Show it."

Marina looked up, met Jules' gaze, and for once—didn't deflect.

PART IV – CLOSING TIME

The lounge was quiet again.

Chairs stacked. Lights dimmed to amber.

Marina locked the door, the sound echoing too loudly in the hollow space. For the first time in a long while, she didn't reach for her phone. Didn't scroll. Didn't busy her hands with something safe.

She stood at the center of the room where Logan had played, eyes closed, hearing faint echoes of the set still circling the walls.

Her pulse matched the rhythm.

She whispered to the empty air—barely audible, but true.

"Another time."

CHAPTER EIGHT: FIRST KISS / NEAR MISS

PART I – LEFT BEHIND

Everyone had gone.

After close, *Ember & Wax* became something else entirely—a cathedral to what was possible. The lounge held its breath in the quiet, the scent of citrus lingering like a ghost of earlier warmth. The only sound was the soft hum of refrigeration and the occasional clink of glassware being polished in the back.

Marina stayed behind, perched on the edge of a velvet booth. Her blazer draped beside her like the husk of a life she kept trying to outgrow.

Her hair was unpinned.

Her heels were off.

She felt... undone.

She wasn't sure how long she'd been sitting there when she sensed someone in the doorway.

"I thought you left," she said, not looking up. Eyes fixed on the low glow of a nearby lamp.

Logan's voice answered, warm but calm. "I almost did."

Marina looked at her.

Silence stretched between them—not awkward, not cold. Just full. The kind of silence that only exists between two people who've stopped pretending they aren't thinking the same thing.

PART II – THE AIR BETWEEN

Logan crossed the room slowly.

Carefully.

Like she didn't want to startle whatever fragile thing had begun to form in the quiet between them.

"You okay?" she asked gently.

Marina hesitated. "No." A quiet laugh slipped out, self-deprecating. "Not logistically. Not emotionally either. Depends on your definition."

Logan gave a slow, crooked smile. "Well. That's honesty. Progress, maybe."

Marina exhaled. "It's not about you."

"Isn't it?"

That hit harder than it should have.

Marina looked up, suddenly.

Logan wasn't smirking. Wasn't pressing.

Just... present.

Without pressure.

Without pretense.

"You scare the hell out of me," Marina said.

It came out like most truths—unbidden and irreversible.

Logan's expression softened instantly.

"I'm not trying to," she said gently.

"I know. That's the problem," Marina whispered. "That's what scares me."

PART III – TRUTH IN THE SHADOWS

They didn't step. They leaned. Like gravity had finally caught up with them. Somehow they were closer now. Not all at once.
Just... there.
Inches apart.

Logan moved in, slow and sure, eyes never leaving Marina's. She placed her palm against Marina's jaw—soft, steady, and anchored.
Marina's breath trembled against Logan's mouth.

There was a heartbeat of hesitation.
A breath-long pause where consent waited and bloomed.

"You don't have to tell anyone," Logan said. "I'm not asking for some big reveal. I'm not here to blow up your life."
"I know that too," Marina said slowly.
"I just don't want to be something you regret."
"You're not," Marina whispered.

They leaned in the last inch together.
The kiss was slow. Certain. Not rushed, not devouring—just real. A consistent heat, learning its way around barriers.

Logan tasted like citrus and something midnight-sweet.

Their mouths moved together in a language neither of them had been taught—but instinct knew.

Tongues touched.
Sighed approval.
Hands found space between fabric and skin.

They didn't speak.
Their bodies did.
And in those moments, Marina opened.
Not because she was ready—because she finally wanted to be.

PART IV – REALITY INTRUDES

The back door slammed.

Avery's voice floated in from the kitchen: "Sorry! Dropped the mop—ghosts in the dish pit again!"

The spell fractured.
Logan pulled back a half-inch.
They both stepped away too quickly—like it burned to stay close any longer.
Their foreheads met briefly—one last press of something unspoken.

Marina's lipstick was smudged. For once, she didn't fix it.

She straightened her shirt.
Breathed. Willed herself still.

Logan didn't rush to speak.
When she did, her voice was soft. "Next time."
Her thumb swept the edge of Marina's cheekbone—light, reverent.

Marina met her gaze. "Next time," she echoed.
Logan nodded once. Then turned and walked away.
But this time, Marina didn't look away.

CHAPTER NINE: B-Story / Found Family

PART I – AFTER HOURS

The last patrons had gone home, and the speakers in *Ember & Wax* hummed with the soft static of silence. Lights dimmed low. The air smelled faintly of orange peel and sandalwood—clean, lived-in, safe.

Jules dragged a chair from the corner, spun it backward, and dropped into it. "All right, survivors. Who's hungry?"

Avery raised a hand without looking up from their phone. "You mean emotionally or literally?"

"Both," Maya said, already kicking a crate of glassware out of the walkway with the toe of her boot. "But we start with carbs."

"Marina? You're staying," Jules declared. "You owe us."

Marina was in mid-inventory, staring at a stack of menus. Glancing over her right shoulder, she said,

"Owe you, what?"

"Our sanity", Avery said, waving a garnish in the air. "You made us change the menu garnish program three times."

"No, four," Maya chimed in. She sported an undercut and a wit sharp enough to slice through tension.

Marina leaned against the bar, watching them move. The laughter was low and uneven, like something rediscovered. Someone turned on the old record player in the corner; soft crackle filled the room before music found its groove.

Jules grinned. "By the way, I ordered pizza. Don't thank me yet —it's from that place with the existential breadsticks." Maya laughed.
"The ones that taste like regret?"
"Exactly."

Maya peeled off a bar towel and slung it over her shoulder. "Regret pairs well with ranch."

The room exhaled. For once, no one was performing.

PART II – THE QUIET BETWEEN

When the pizza arrived, it came in too many boxes and not enough napkins. They ate standing, sitting, sprawled—half of them in the wrong chairs, the way families always do. Marina stayed on the edge of it at first, watching the way everyone filled space without asking permission.

Jules teasing Avery about their playlist. Maya sliding into whatever task appeared and finishing it without fanfare. Someone— probably Jules—had written QUEER FUEL in Sharpie on the lid.

The laughter came easy.
Too easy.

Marina tried to join it, but something about the simplicity of it all felt fragile—like glass between her fingers. Maya caught Marina watching.

"You're allowed to sit," she said, not unkindly, nodding toward the center of the mess. Marina blinked. "I am sitting," Marina offered, still half-perched on the edge of the bar.

Maya tilted her head.

"No. Here." She tapped the cushion beside her. "With us."

Something in the phrasing loosened a knot. Marina hesitated, then crossed the room.

She sat.

The conversation shifted around her, gently making space as if it had always known where she fit. Avery leaned against her shoulder mid-story like it was the most natural thing in the world. Jules reached over to refill Marina's glass without asking. Maya, she slid a napkin onto Marina's knee—practical, wordless, seen.

Something inside her settled. Quietly.

PART III – THE STORY GAME

They talked in spirals of jokes, half-told stories, running in-jokes that tangled and teased. Not excluding her—not entirely—but weaving her in, slowly.

"Okay. Wait," Jules said, mouth full of crust. "New rule," Jules announced. "Weirdest job you ever had."

Avery shot up a hand. "Disneyland parade dancer. Mickey's Halloween cavalcade. Tail was a hazard."

"Artistic sacrifice," Jules intoned.

Maya wiped pizza grease from her fingers. "I did wig styling at a strip-mall salon for three months. Learned more about physics than in high school."

Avery perked up. "Explain."
"High ponytails are structural engineering," Maya said. "Load-bearing scrunchies." Laughter tumbled through the room.

Marina hesitated.

"I... worked front desk at a gym."

They all looked at her. Jules smirked. "You? Telling people where the towels are?"

"I quit after three days."
"Why?"

Marina took a long sip of her drink.

"Because they tried to make me lead Zumba."

The room broke into laughter that rolled and spilled, soft and genuine.

Avery conducted the room to silence, waving a breadstick like a conductor's baton.

"Wait, wait, wait. Switch, new story."

"Oh God," Jules groaned.

Avery turned to Maya and said, "Tell Marina about the last Pride."

Marina turned toward Maya with curiosity all over her face and mouthed, *the last Pride?*

"OMG!! It was an accident!" Maya protested.

"You threw a dildo at a mounted cop," Jules said, dramatically.

"He was asking for it," Maya shot back, unapologetic.

"Literally or—?" Jules teased. "Both," Maya smirked.

Marina laughed again—a real laugh, not measured, not guarded. It startled her. She hadn't done that in months.

Maybe longer.

PART IV – THE WARM DOWN

An hour later, the boxes were empty. The air felt heavier, as if it had absorbed their warmth. Jules stretched like a cat. Avery contemplated stealing the last crust. Maya folded lids into neat flats and stacked them by the door.

"Remind me to never eat that much again," she murmured.

"Remind me to stop you," Jules said. Avery yawned, stretching dramatically. "Remind me to ghost everyone and take leftovers."

Maya flicked a glance at Marina, soft with humor. "Remind me to label the breadsticks 'acceptance issues'."

They all laughed again.

After the room settled back into the quiet humming, Marina broke the silence.

"You're not what I expected," Marina said softly.
Avery and Maya looked at her questionably. Jules tilted their head. "And what did you expect?"

Marina toyed with the rim of her glass.

"A walking HR violation."

Jules leaned back, arm draped over the couch. "I contain multitudes." They sipped. Then Jules looked at Marina more sharply.

"You like her, don't you?"
Marina tensed. "Who?"
"Please," Jules said, gentler now.

Avery and Maya leaned in with suspense. Marina looked down at her lap. Nails pristine. No chips. No color. Control everywhere.
Then—

"It's complicated."
Jules laughed—soft, warm. "It's only complicated if you keep pretending it isn't happening."
Marina looked up, meeting Jules's eyes. "You make it sound easy."
"I make it sound worth it," Jules replied. "That's different."

Marina looked at them—their half-eaten crusts, their messy laughter, the way no one here seemed to need armor. She wasn't sure what she felt. But she knew what it wasn't.

It wasn't fear.
It wasn't distance.
It was something close to home.

PART V – LOCKING UP

When the others left, Marina stayed behind again. She cleared the tables slowly, her movements unhurried. The citrus scent still lingered; sandalwood deeper now, like the night had exhaled with her. She ran her hand along the back of the booth where she'd sat earlier—where laughter had settled into memory. She noticed a faint dark ring from a sweating glass marked the vinyl. She pressed her palm over it and felt the cool.

For once, she didn't feel like a guest in her own space.
The silence that followed wasn't empty.
It was full.

CHAPTER TEN: ROMANCE HEATS UP

PART I – MIDNIGHT SESSION

———————

The text came just after midnight.

Logan: *You still awake?*

Marina stared at it in the dark.

Marina: *Barely. Why?*
Logan: *I need to test the levels. Could use your ears.*
Marina: *Now?*
Logan: *Now's honest. Come if you want.*

She hesitated. **"Come if you want"** felt like a door cracking open.

Marina chose it.

Reached for her keys.

PART II – EMBER AFTER DARK

The lounge was different at this hour.

12:17 a.m. — all hush and promise.

No music.
No chatter.
Just shadows and silence and the soft pulse of the exit sign over the back door.

Logan stood at the booth, grey hoodie, sweatsuit, hair tied back.
Marina let the door close behind her.

"You were serious about this sound check?" Logan glanced at her with a grin on her face. "That's what got you here, right?"

Marina smiled, small and tight. "Mostly."

Logan gestured toward the riser.

"I wanted you to hear something."

She cued a private track: warm synths, heartbeat percussion, and a vinyl hiss that felt like skin on silk.

"I wrote it the night I met you," Logan said. "After we semi-kissed. And for when we finally did." As her mouth slowly curved.

The beat moved slowly—slower than usual. No vocals. Just warm synths and low textures. Music made for eye contact and unspoken truths that have been avoided.

Marina blinked. "You made a whole track about me?"
"I made a whole track about what it felt like not to look away."

The music swelled. Not dramatic—intimate. Like someone whispering a secret you weren't supposed to hear.

Marina's chest tightened.

"I don't know what I'm doing," she said softly.
"Let's remember together," Logan replied.

PART III – THE KISS

They didn't step closer. They fell.
One second Marina was blinking through the weight of what was in the air. Then next, Logan's hand was on her jaw, and their mouths met like they'd done it a thousand times in a thousand quiet rooms just like this. They met like they remembered how.

Logan's hand bracketed Marina's hip. Marina's fingers threaded the soft tumble of curls at Logan's nape and pulled her closer. The kiss deepened—patiently, slowly turning to hunger, composed shifting to mine. Remembering where they had left off the first time they kissed.

Logan grinned against Marina's quiet, startled sound.
It wasn't frantic.

It wasn't wild.

It was sure. Earned.

Marina inhaled sharply but didn't pull back.

Logan's breath warmed her cheek. Consent wasn't a box; it was a rhythm.

Marina matched it.

She let it happen.

She let herself stay.

Not for control.

Not for retreat.

Just... to be.

Logan broke the kiss, but their foreheads remained touching, breath shallow and mingled—Marina stayed still.

She didn't reach for her blazer.

She didn't reach for her rules.

She stayed.

Eyes closed.

Breathing uneven.

Fingers became cartographers of heat and hunger. Fabric whispered against skin, surrendering to the slow, assured slide of discovery. Cool air kissed exposed skin in gentle contrast to the warmth blooming between them.

They moved to the front of the riser.

The baseline throbbed through the floor, vibrating up through the soles of their feet. The back of Marina's knees introduced a new pulse that orchestrated her body to a new place.

Marina climbed into Logan's lap with effortless gravity. She wrapped her legs around Logan's like her life depended on it.

The blazer slipped off the riser, a hush of cloth against the polished concrete floor.

Their mouths met again—pulse for pulse, breath for breath—each kiss syncopated with the rhythm swelling around them.

Kiss, breath, laugh, kiss again.

Logan's hands anchored at Marina's waist, her thumbs drawing slowly—circling hypnotically beneath the hem of silk. Marina leaned into the touch, spine bowing in a fluid arc, surrendering not from weakness, but from choice. The kind of control that blooms only when permission meets desire.

"You okay?" Logan murmured, voice husky with care, gaze searching. "I'm here," Marina said. Her breath hitched into the words, "don't stop."

And she meant it.
Now, everything was open—
No barriers.
No hesitation.
Just skin, breath, the delicious ache of building pressure—sensation.

They took their time.
Lingering in the quiet thunder of anticipation. Fingertips explored like music—soft tremolos along the ribcage, chords struck gently where breath caught and deepened. Heat bloomed across Marina's nape. The sensation, a slow fuse of need traveling from

around her neck to her collarbone, sculpting her shoulders down to her fingertips. She felt it from her navel to the base of her spine.

Her hands roamed, mapping Logan's back, learning its contours, sending shivers with every tentative stroke.

Logan's hands mirrored the pace, the pressure—a rhythm neither frantic nor passive, but inevitable.

A new tempo began to build, one composed in the hidden places of touch. Their bodies played it together. Every inhale—part of the composition. Every gasp—a chorus.

Marina's skin glowed with the rising crescendo, her heartbeat syncing with Logan's—thud for thud, like a club track felt through the chest.

Logan paused, eyes locked on Marina. Their breathing stayed in rhythm—same tempo, same fire. And in that quiet between movements, Logan saw it: *Marina wanted her. Bad.* The need wasn't subtle. It was in her eyes—the hunger, the ache, the silent— *Yes.*

She ached.
And Logan? She was right there with her.

"I need you on the riser," Logan whispered.

Marina did not blink. Without a word, she adjusted—smooth, sure, shifting her body without breaking rhythm, without letting go. She moved like she already knew what Logan needed. Climbed into position like she was made for it.

Logan bit down a moan, grinning through it. A flash of admiration cut through the heat. *Damn, she's flexible. So present.*

No hesitation. No shame. Just heat and trust and motion.

Logan grinned again, then kissed her way down—jaw, neck, clavicle—each one slow, deliberate, *reverent.*

Until—

She finally arrived at the place where breath stalled and bodies arched.

Marina melted into her, back curving, hands gripping Logan's shoulders as sweat began to gather at their spines, *slick* and *sweet.*

The wave crested between them. Logan, though it had been a while, remembered this language—the way need spoke without sound, the way desire made time bend. Logan kissed her way lower to the center of heat and tension and unraveling.

Marina felt the moment.
Logan felt the shift.

The energy coiled and hummed.

Logan reached for it, for Marina's rhythm, and touched gently —finding the pulse with a featherlight circle.

Not rushed.
Not tentative.
Just knowing.

And then, like a DJ on a dimly lit stage, Logan cued the drop. Two fingers entered the mix—confidently, slowly, controlled— turned the tempo with precision. Logan felt a pulse beneath her touch. Marina's moan broke through the haze like a sampled vocal echoing in an empty warehouse.

And Logan kept at it—cutting, cueing, building.
Cut.
Cue.
Cut... and cue.

Marina's breath faltered with each stroke. Her grip on Logan's back slipped again and again—slick now with sweat, but firm in need. They moved together, chasing that last, inevitable crescendo. And when it came, it wasn't a scream or a gasp.

It was a stillness.
A silence so thick it sang.

They stilled, foreheads pressed once more. Chests rose and fell in sync. The room around them seemed rewired—every surface hummed with what had passed between them. Even the acoustics seemed to lean in, amplifying the quiet beat of their shared breath, wrapped around them like a lullaby of rhythm and release.

For once, Marina didn't reach for control.
She just breathed.

And it didn't feel like failure.

PART IV – AFTERMATH

They sat on the riser afterward, legs touching. Logan reached into her bag and passed her a bottle of water.

Neither of them spoke—silence stretched comfortably.

"I've never..." Marina began.

Logan waited.

"...let anyone see me like this. Not like that."

Logan leaned her head back, eyes on the ceiling, while her thumb traced circles over Marina's knuckles.

"You looked like yourself."
"I did."

The words sat heavy—true.
Marina didn't apologize for them.

Logan kept thumbing circles over her knuckles.

CHAPTER ELEVEN: MIDPOINT
(False High)

PART I – GLOW

Marina walked into *Ember & Wax* three hours before doors opened, and everyone noticed something had changed.

She was light on her feet, and it showed.
Her blouse was silk instead of starched. Lipstick had a slight sheen. A smile that reached all the way through her.

Jules clocked it in one glance. Avery slid her a cortado with a knowing, "Finally."

"You get laid or won the lotto?" Jules asked, deadpan.

Marina didn't flinch.
"Maybe both," she said.

Avery gave a slow, dramatic bow behind the bar.
Maya whispered, "Power move," and slid her a second cortado.

PART II – THE INVITE

Logan showed up later that afternoon, gear bag over her shoulder, sunglasses perched in her curls. Marina didn't hide the smile that bloomed the second Logan walked in—sunlight where night used to live.

"Didn't think I'd see you in the daylight," Marina teased.
"Careful," Logan said. "Flirting's dangerous."
"For whom?"

Logan stepped in, close. Real close. "For whoever has to go home alone tonight."

Marina blushed. Visibly.
It made her laugh.

They tucked into the back booth to review the tech run for the grand opening. Halfway through, Logan closed the laptop.

"I have an idea," she said.
Marina raised an eyebrow. "Should I be scared?"
"A little," Logan grinned. "I want you to spin the last track with me."
Marina blinked.
"Me?"
"You said you used to mix in college, right?"
"That was... another lifetime."
"You still have hands, right?"

It landed like an invitation and a dare.

Marina snorted. Looking down at her hands, she retorted, "Do I?!"

Logan couldn't help but laugh. Then Marina said, "But what if I mess it up?" Logan leaned forward, eyes unwavering. "Then we mess it up together."

Logan had a big smile on her face. Marina laughed into the kiss they stole behind a partition and said, "If I trip, you catch me?"

"Every time," Logan said.

Not romantic—just true.

And both of them smiled like they believed it.

PART III – MAGIC IN THE BOOTH

They stayed after hours again that night.

Marina stood behind the booth, fingers hovering over sliders, headset half on.

"You're overthinking it," Logan said.

"I don't like surprises."

"You are one," Logan murmured with her mouth against Marina's temple.

Marina looked at her. "I mean it," Logan said. "You walk through this place like you built it. But I think there's something even better waiting on the other side of scared."

The words lodged somewhere deep inside her. The room seemed to hold its breath with her.

They practiced. Marina on fader, Logan guiding her wrist. The intimacy of learning replaced performance. Trust layered beneath their hands.

And they dropped the track.

Together.

PART IV – CAUGHT IN THE LIGHT

The night before the grand opening, Marina lay in bed with her phone beside her. The glow of Logan's playlist lit up her bedroom wall. Every track felt like a secret.

One played on loop.

A remix Logan hadn't published. A track built around breath and heartbeat. It felt like falling into something.

And—for the first time—it didn't feel like drowning.

CHAPTER TWELVE: THE LIE HITS BACK

PART I – EXPOSURE

The photo wasn't scandalous.
Not in the way tabloids foamed over.
No kissing.
No skin.
No drama.
Just a moment—frozen under warm lighting—Marina's hand rested lightly on Logan's forearm. Both laughing. Not posed. Just present. And maybe... too at ease.

Jules reposted it to the lounge's Instagram story:

@emberwaxlounge

Behind-the-scenes chaos. You'll want to hear the final set. 

It only lived for forty-eight hours, but that was long enough.
By noon, Marina's phone had pinged three times with the same preview:
Mom.

PART II – THE CALL

She took the call in her office, door shut, AC hummed like a warning.

Her mother's voice was clipped. Careful. Like she rehearsed a line she didn't want to say but felt obligated to deliver.

"I saw something."

Marina's fingers froze on the edge of her laptop.

"What kind of something?" She asked, even though she knew.
"A photo. You were... touching someone."

There was a pause. Not a dramatic one. A disappointed one. The kind that wounds without raising its voice.

"She's the DJ, isn't she? The one Ryan said was inappropriate?"

Marina closed her eyes. The air thickened like smoke from a 5-alarm fire.

"I don't care what Ryan said."
"You're not denying it."
"I'm not confirming anything either."
"That's not good enough, Marina."

That sentence. Sharp. Final.
Marina stared at her reflection in her dark laptop screen.

"Is this how you want to be seen?" her mother asked softly.

And there it was.
Not: *What do you feel? Or are you happy?*
Just: **How will others perceive you?**

Marina's voice, when it finally came, cracked under the weight of restraint.

"I want to be honest."

Silence.
Then the line went dead.

PART III – PANIC MODE

―――――――――

She tried to work. Tried to focus on anything but the fact that her mother had hung up without saying goodbye.

Inventory counts blurred. Menu edits became gibberish. Fifty-six emails blinked unread like a wall of silent accusations.

Her mouse shook in her grip.
Her phone buzzed again.
This time she jumped.

Jules walked by the open door, paused, and moved on without a word. Jules was near the ice machine now.
Avery whispered, "Let her process."

Marina read the message.
She typed to reply to Logan.

Deleted it.
Typed again.
Deleted it again.

She could feel the distance between them—real or imagined—was unbearable. She shut off her phone and placed it face down like it was radioactive.

PART IV – EMPTY SPACES

That night, ***Ember & Wax*** was packed. Stylish regulars laughed and clinked glasses under golden light. Every seat was full.

But it all felt... hollow.

Logan wasn't in the booth. The stage lights flickered without meaning. The spot where Logan usually stood felt like it was waiting.

Marina lingered near the service station, watching the emptiness like it might explain itself.

Someone bumped her shoulder. She barely noticed.

Jules caught her eye from across the room. Worried, maybe. Or just waiting.

Marina straightened. Smoothed her blazer.

But inside, the song she'd hummed all week—Logan's track, the one that once sounded like falling—

Now rang cold.

Distant.

Like something she wasn't sure she'd ever hear again.

CHAPTER THIRTEEN: CRISIS MOMENT

PART I – THE SETUP

The air inside *Ember & Wax* buzzed with quiet tension — conversation layered with ambition, ambition cloaked as socializing. It was industry night: restaurant owners, lighting gurus, cocktail consultants, and the usual parade of influencers with ring lights and half-empty expectations.

Marina walked in wearing all black. Silk blouse muted. Hair twisted into a sleek knot. No lipstick. No softness. Just armor.

She hadn't seen Logan in four days.

But she knew Logan was supposed to be here. Jules had hinted at a "surprise set."

She told herself it didn't matter.

PART II – RYAN RETURNS

Ryan arrived like a storm disguised as weather.

He slid up to the bar, ordered something smoky, eyes darting toward Marina.

"Hey, stranger."

"Leave." Her voice was sharp, cold.

He raised his glass. "You never responded to my message."

She didn't flinch. "You, should not be here."

"I was invited," he replied, nodding toward a PR contact.

He stepped in closer, voice dropping. "I saw the photo. Nice work, by the way. Very... ambiguous."

Marina's jaw tightened. She raised one finger, sliced the air like a blade. Her voice didn't rise.

"Don't! Fuck with me."

He caught the edge of her gaze and softened his tone—just a shade. "Don't what? Ask questions? Or tell the truth?"

She stared.

He smiled and pushed it further. "Everyone's whispering."

His voice lifted. "You might as well confirm it."

The music dipped.

Voices quieted.

Her heart stuttered.

Then—

Ryan's voice cut cleanly through the hush.

"So what is she, Marina? Just a phase? Or are we all supposed to pretend you haven't been lying for years?"

PART III – THE SHATTER

Silence fractured like a tree struck by lightning — instant destruction wrapped in stunned awe.

In the distance, a tray hit the floor. Glass met tile behind the bar, in a shattering kiss—loud and final.

Sporadically, multiple people gasped.

Marina's breath clogged her throat.
She couldn't speak.
Because Logan was there now. At the back of the room near the booth, Logan stood — still.

Protective distance.
Hurt carved across her face.
Not anger.
Just... stillness.
Marina watched Logan retreat.

The world shrank with every footfall taken.

PART IV – FALLOUT

Jules emerged first. Then Avery.
No jokes.
No comfort.
Just a steady presence.

One of them said softly, "Come."
Marina shook her head.
Her voice barely made it out. "No."
Without looking back, she walked straight through the staff exit.

Into the alley.
Into the night.
No tears.
No scene.
Just emptiness.
And the sound of her own silence, loud as grief.

CHAPTER FOURTEEN: BREAK-UP / DARK NIGHT

PART I – LOCKED DOORS

The lounge was open—doors unlocked, lights warm—but Marina was not.

Six days had passed.

She hadn't answered texts. Ignored calls. Skipped the final sound checks for the grand opening.

Jules covered. Avery lied. Maya told a brand rep she had the flu.
But no one believed that.

She was present only in tasks—in inventory, in spreadsheets, in logistics—but absent from the place she had built with precision and fear.

She was not here.
Not really.
She hadn't touched the booth. Hadn't touched music.
Hadn't touched anything that reminded her of Logan.

PART II – LOGAN SHOWS UP

It was too early for customers when Marina entered the lounge. She expected emptiness.

Instead, Logan was there—hood down, headphones slung around her neck like a weight she hadn't decided to carry or let go.

A breath snagged in Marina's chest. The scent of bergamot, vinyl, and something softer hit her nose—left behind once, now returned like a memory–Logan's hoodie.

"You're not answering me," Logan said. Her voice was steady. Not cold.

Marina's gaze dropped. "I can't do this right now."

Logan stepped closer. "Tough."

Marina swallowed.

"I didn't ask for this. Any of this. I didn't want it to unravel like this."

"And yet it did."

Marina's voice sharpened. "Do you know what it's like to watch everything you built unravel in a second?"

Logan didn't flinch.

"Yes," she said. "Because I built it too. And I chose not to lie."

PART III – THE TRUTH, FINALLY

Logan's words dropped between them like thunder muffled by velvet.

"I came out at nineteen. My mother cried for weeks. My uncle called me disgusting. Half of my friends disappeared like they'd never existed. But, I did it anyway. Because living as someone else? That's not living. Not, an option!!"

Marina looked down. Couldn't speak.
So Logan did.

"You think hiding keeps you safe. It doesn't. It keeps you small. It keeps you alone. It keeps you numb."
Marina's voice cracked. "It's not that easy."
"I never said it was easy. I said it was worth it."

A silence deeper than music filled the lounge—dense and pressing, the kind of silence that once felt like safety, now pressed into Marina's ribs like armor turned to stone.

"You kissed me like you meant it," Logan said. "And I believed you."
She paused.
"But I won't stay here, waiting for you to erase that."
She turned toward the riser. The booth where silence had given way to something louder.

"I'm playing the grand opening," she said. "But not with you."
Then she walked out.

And this time, she didn't look back.

PART IV – ALONE

Marina didn't cry.

She stood there, motionless, in the center of her carefully curated life.

In the hush of a lounge designed to let others breathe, she finally realized—

She couldn't live here anymore.
Not like this.
Not half-hers.

She closed her eyes. Feeling her chest rise and fall. Behind her eyelids, she saw Logan's hands guiding her through that last track. Felt the baseline still waiting to drop.

And somewhere in the silence, her fingers flexed.
Not to let go.
To reach for something else.
Maybe for herself.

CHAPTER FIFTEEN: RALLY

PART I – STILLNESS

Marina didn't go home that night.
Instead, she stayed at *Ember & Wax* after closing.
The lights were dimmed.

After last call, long after the final voice faded, she locked the door with shaking fingers and let the silence envelop her. Her phone was already turned off.

She kicked off her heels at the door. The click of them falling echoed–sharp, intrusive. Her wrinkled blazer that carried traces of Logan's perfume from *that* night slipped from her shoulders and landed in a heap by the couch. She curled herself onto one of the velvet sofas—the burgundy one where they'd once kissed against during a closing shift, laughter muffled between mouthfuls of want.

Now... it felt colder.
Distant. A stage after the curtain dropped.
The lounge was silent.
No conversations. No jazz threading through the air. No candlelight flickering in eyes.

Just her.
Her fingers ghosted the rim of a forgotten wine glass.
Her body ached—not from work or desire, but from the hollowness that followed both.
She wanted to cry, but couldn't.

She wanted to scream, but didn't.
She just existed.
Unmoving. Unhealed.
Until—

The door clicked.
A slow, deliberate turn of the lock.

PART II – THEY SHOWED UP

Jules entered first.
Thai takeout in one hand, six-pack of fancy ginger beer in the other. Eyes full of exhausted devotion and the kind of irritation only love excuses.

Behind them, Avery—always calm, steady—holding a plush blanket that smelled faintly of cedar-wood and rose.
And then Maya.
Maya with her Bluetooth speaker blasting Mitski at half-volume, unapologetic as always.

"You didn't answer our texts," Jules said, setting everything down.

Their voice was soft but carried the weight of knowing.

"I didn't want company," Marina whispered, hoarse from silence.

"Too bad," Avery replied, wrapping the blanket over Marina's shoulders with the ease of someone who's done it a hundred times.

The warmth startled her. The fabric brushed her bare thighs. Skin met skin when Avery's fingers brushed hers—long enough to register the chill she hadn't noticed.

Maya plopped onto the floor, cross-legged, her hoodie half unzipped and exposing a sliver of tattooed hip.

"You think you invented queer heartbreak?" she asked with a grin. "Please. I got dumped by a mime once. A mime, Marina."

A laugh escaped Marina before she could stop it. Just a breath— but it cracked through the air like lightning.

They didn't crowd her.
Didn't pry.
They let her come back in fragments.
And they stayed, chaotic and intentional, forming a circle of softness around her like sentinels.

PART III – REAL TALK, AGAIN

Time passed. Takeout cooled.
Cushions shifted as bodies relaxed.
The room filled with the scent of spices, sandalwood, and shared memory. Maya's playlist looped softly with slow queer ballads —songs that stung and soothed at once.

Jules broke the silence.
"You don't have to come out to everyone."

They dipped a spring roll in sauce without looking up.
"But you do have to stop hiding from yourself."

Their words landed like a hand on the small of her back—steady, sure.

Avery stretched out on the couch beside Marina, their legs brushing. The warmth of their leg lingered against hers.

"You can't love anyone if you're scared of your own reflection," they said.

Marina didn't answer right away.
Instead, her eyes flicked to the tiny candle that Maya had lit on the bar top. The soft flicker illuminated their faces.
Her people—her chosen family.

"I don't know how to fix it," she said at last, voice raw.
"You don't," Maya replied, sipping ginger beer through a straw. "You just show up different."

That stuck—*Show up different.*
Not bigger.
Not better.
Just... more honest.
More hers.

PART IV – THE CHOICE BEGINS

They didn't say: fight for her.
They didn't say: go get Logan back.
They didn't need to.

Because Logan—beautiful, brilliant, complicated, aching—had been the spark.

...But this, this *fire?* This *undoing?*
It had *never* been about Logan.
It had *always* been about Marina.

Her reflection in the mirror after undressing.
The way she kissed with her eyes wide open.
The way she held back, even when she was being held.

And now, here—barefoot and blanketed, with her head against Avery's shoulder, Jules's fingers occasionally brushing hers as they passed a carton back and forth, Maya sprawled out with her head in Marina's lap—

Now—
It was evident—

It was about choice.
Whether Marina was finally ready to stop running from the want stitched into her bones.

She looked at them—loyal, messy, loud, alive.

They had already chosen her.
Every time.

Maybe it was time she did, too.

CHAPTER SIXTEEN: BIG GESTURE

PART I – DOORS OPEN

The grand opening shimmered.

It wasn't just successful—it seduced.

Every table full. Every corner lit like desire in motion. Walls whispered secrets. Light traced collarbones and glinted off polished glass.

Ember & Wax looked like a fantasy someone dared to manifest—lush, expensive, almost obscene in its intimacy. The city's most curated creatures had come to worship: influencers, editors, DJs, exes.

Everyone wanted in.

And Marina?

She stood in the mezzanine, one manicured hand pressed hard to the brass railing, the other gripping her phone like a talisman, trying not to crumble in her heels. Her heart pounded between her ribs like it wanted out. Her breathing caught—shallow, ragged. Lipstick perfect. Silk jumpsuit clung to her body like it knew every curve.

But still—her hands shook.

"Are you sure?" Jules's voice came, velvet-soft beside her.

Marina looked up, eyes rimmed with anxiety and waterproof mascara. "No."

"Good," Jules said. "That means it matters."

PART II – THE WALK

She walked down the steps out onto the floor up onto the stage like a woman stepping off a ledge. Her heels introduced her to the crowd.

The lounge dipped into a hush.

Her presence roared. Every gaze followed. She moved slowly, deliberately—hips swaying, face neutral, eyes locked on the mic like it was a lifeline.

Avery gave a small nod from the booth.

Maya, off to the side, turned the music down to a slow pulse—ambient, teasing. Lights dimmed to molten amber, wrapping Marina in a golden flush.

She gripped the mic with both hands. Her fingers tightened around it like it might steady her.

"I built this place so people could breathe," she began, her voice low, steady, intimate. "A place where people can be free...even when I couldn't."

She paused.
The silence pressed in, heavy and expectant.

"But tonight," she exhaled sharply, voice vibrating, "I'm choosing to breathe in it."

A heartbeat passed.
Then another.

"I want to say something before the final set."

Her eyes scanned the crowd. Crystal glasses. Velvet coaches. *The Amythest VIP* section was full. Cameras ready to rise and capture the moment. Her mother—front and center—flawless in pearls, unreadable.

"Some of you know me as the owner here. Some of you know me as someone else entirely."

Murmurs stirred. Champagne clinked. A camera flashed.

"I spent years curating perfection—
Smooth edges.
Silences.
Shadows."

Another breath. *The truth climbed up her throat like fire.*

"But it is time I am free. The truth is—I'm in love with the woman about to take the stage."

It dropped like a *storm.* The room exploded.
Gasps. Laughter. A burst of applause began—staggered, uncertain.

And THEN—

Her mother stood abruptly.

Her chair scraped the polished charcoal concrete floor with a long, slow exhale of disapproval.

Her jaw was set like stone.

Her eyes met Marina's—fierce, wounded, cold.

Marina felt the ache bloom sharply—instantly. A thorn buried deep in her heart.

She didn't move.

Another flash.

Another breath.

Marina didn't waver.

Her mother didn't speak.

She gathered her purse.

Turned.

Walked out.

Marina watched her go without breaking.

Not numb.

Just choosing.

PART III – STAYING STILL

She didn't follow.

Didn't cry.

Didn't fold.

Instead, she let the ache breathe.

Let it pulse.

Let it live.

Across the room, Logan stood frozen behind the DJ booth. Her hand still gripped the vinyl. Her mouth parted, eyes wide—astonishment, not fear.

Marina stepped off the stage. Each step was a slow burn—heels clicking against the concrete floor, breath syncing with her heartbeat, gaze never leaving Logan's.

The crowd parted around her like a benediction.

Phones raised.

She didn't shrink.

She walked right up to the booth. Took Logan's hand.

And kissed her.

Not timid.

Not polite or performatively.

A full-bodied kiss. Lips parted. Tongue slipping slowly against Logan's lip, drawing a soft gasp from Logan's throat. Marina gripped Logan's waist with one hand and tilted her jaw with the other, just so. Commanding the space like it was hers.

The room erupted.

It wasn't just applause—it was release. The noise—applause, screams—crashed over them like that perfect ocean tide.

Jules shouted above it all, near tears. Avery whistled loudly as if they were at a basketball game. Maya, of course, yelled, *"YES, YES, YES,"* like it was a battle cry—phone held high.

Logan's fingers tangled into Marina's hair, tugging just enough to make her moan softly into the kiss.

They broke apart, breathless.
Marina laughed, flushed and radiant, unbothered at the chaos or the flashing lights.

"Play it," she whispered into Logan's mouth, lips brushing.
"Are you sure?" Logan asked, voice rough with affection and something darker.
"I'm done hiding," Marina said, voice low and burning. "Play our track."

Logan smiled—a smile laced with reverence and wickedness. She slid
behind the booth, hands precise and fast. The music surged— the mix they'd made on that drunken night months ago, half-naked on the floor, fingers sticky with honey and bass.

The beat dropped.
Slow. Wet. Hot.
The speakers moaned with low, vibrating synths that curled into your hips. The bass pulsed like a second heartbeat. Lights arced through the fog in hues of peach and gold.

Marina didn't move away.
She stayed.

Pressed against Logan's side, arm wrapped possessively around her waist. Fingers tracing idle lines along the dip of Logan's back, where her spine met her hips.

They swayed—bodies warm, sweat forming at the nape of Marina's neck, lips brushing Logan's shoulder.

Not dancing—communing.

A slow ritual of bodies that had nothing to prove, only remember.

Around them, the room pulsed. Friends tangled. Lovers touched. Bodies surrendered. Eyes glistened.

Every camera caught it.

Marina—head thrown back in a full laugh, arms stretched around a woman she refused to lose again.

She was radiant.

Unapologetic.

Alive.

And this time, she didn't care who watched.

CHAPTER SEVENTEEN: CLIMAX

PART I – THE DROP

———

Logan's set didn't just slap.
It seduced.
It growled.
It undressed the room.

The first drop shuddered up from the subwoofers and into every hip, every collarbone, every parted mouth. *Ember & Wax* transformed—from a curated lounge into something more primal.
Something sweaty.
Urgent.
Alive.

The bass became breath. The rhythm became law.
Bodies collided in time—mouths brushed, limbs tangled, dresses rode up, shirts unbuttoned halfway—both heat and hunger. Touch everywhere. Heat beaded at brows, lips slick with champagne or someone else's gloss. The room moaned with it.

Marina wasn't just in the crowd.
She was part of it.
Her fingers laced with Logan's, pulled tight so they wouldn't lose each other in the thrum. The clutch of their hands wasn't just romantic—it was need—a tether. A promise.

Marina and Logan left the booth and joined the crowd on the floor. Every few beats, someone leaned into Marina's space with a grin:

"*Thank you.*"

"Beautiful."

"About damn time."

A stranger even kissed Marina's cheek like a benediction and disappeared into the press of bodies.

Marina moved to the hallway near the bar as Logan returned to the booth. She scanned the room; this time, no anxiety.

Just freedom.

Jules found her first—grabbed her hand and pulled her—zero patience. "You don't get to give speeches like that and then brood in a corner," they scolded, dragging her toward the vibrating heart of the room.

Avery spun past like a celestial mass, hips sharp, eyes soft. Maya was already twirling a terrified-looking new intern with glitter on their cheeks and confusion in their bones.

A champagne bottle exploded in a spray behind the bar. Someone shouted something joyous in French. Marina threw her head back and laughed—not polite. Not filtered. It tore from her like fire, like flight, like birth. She had waited years to sound like this. For once, she didn't touch her face. Didn't shrink from the eyes.

She just laughed.

Loud. Messy. Holy.

A camera flash captured Marina mid-laugh, eyes closed—Logan in the background staring at her like a woman starving.

By midnight, the photo hit **@emberwaxlounge** with a simple caption:

"The night we caught fire 🔥 💨"

When Marina saw it, she didn't move to edit it. She didn't ask for the filter to be fixed or the narrative shaped.

She just let it be.
Let herself exist.
Let it all unfold—wild and untamed.

PART II – SPOTLIGHT MOMENT

The music built and broke and built again, layers crashing over the crowd like a sensual baptism.
Then—

Logan slowed it.
A hush. Just a low hum of synth under the skin. It felt like the whole room was holding its breath, sweat and tension kissing every surface.

Logan's voice melted through the speakers:
"This track is for Marina."

The reaction wasn't applause—it was sound breaking apart from emotion.

Roars. Screams. Cheers that cracked the glass.

Jules whooped. Maya screamed, "LET'S GOOO." Avery blew her a kiss across the crowd.

Marina covered her face, breath hitching. It was too much. Too good. But she didn't retreat. She dropped her hands.

She laughed again—this time through tears.

Logan's eyes never left hers. Even from across the room, Marina felt the heat of her gaze—a private promise made public. No shame. No holding back.

Logan lifted a hand and beckoned. Come here.

Marina moved.

Each step carved out with electric grace. The crowd parted instinctively—like they knew this was something sacred.

She climbed into the booth.

Her breath trembled.

Logan didn't kiss her—yet.

She just touched her.

Headphones first, sliding them over Marina's ears with slow precision, fingers brushing her temple. Then a soft graze of her knuckles down the curve of Marina's neck—where sweat pooled and pulse pounded. Logan's lips barely brushed her earlobe. "Your turn."

A gasp caught in Marina's throat. Her hands trembled, but she didn't pull away.

She dropped the fader.

Logan guided her wrist like they had rehearsed in private, months ago, bodies pressed together in a sound studio, breath thick with lust and reverb.

Only now, the room was watching.
And it turned them on.

The track surged to life under Marina's touch—seamless and sensual, rising like sex and prophecy.

The drop landed.
Hard.
The room exploded.
Confetti fell from nowhere—like the air couldn't handle the tension and had to break. Champagne sprayed. Someone screamed in catharsis.

Marina didn't flinch.
She was drunk on sound, the sweat, the wildness, the way Logan's hand never left her lower back.
Their eyes locked.
The world roared around them.
They kissed again—longer this time. *Messier.*

Logan's hand slipped just under the hem of Marina's top. Hips grinding against each other like no one could see.
But everyone saw.
No one looked away.
Because this wasn't scandal.
This was **liberation**.

PART III – FINAL BEAT

As the final track slowed and melted into golden hush, Marina stepped down from the booth. Logan at her side.

The crowd surged forward. Applause thundered. Flashes flared.

But all Marina heard was Logan's breath beside her. All she felt was want—steady, burning, true.

She wasn't hiding.

She wasn't surviving anymore.

She was choosing.

And this—

This was how it *began*.

CHAPTER EIGHTEEN: RESOLUTION

PART I – EMBER & WAX, MORNING

The city held its breath at dawn.

The streets were hushed, bathed in that rare golden silence only early morning could conjure—before coffee shops opened, before traffic clawed its way into the day, before the world remembered who it was supposed to be.

Marina unlocked *Ember & Wax* with slow fingers.

The metal gave way like a secret shared. She stepped inside barefoot, heels dangling from one hand like an afterthought. The other hand clutched her silenced phone since last night's firestorm of love and liberation. Her hair was a little ruined—sex-tousled, wind-kissed, sleep-creased. Logan's hoodie swallowed her, warm and too big, with a faint trace of smoke, DJ booth sweat, and desire still etched into the fabric.

The lounge was still recovering from the night before. Champagne stains on the floor. Glitter in the corners. A single bra left on a velvet chair. The scent hung heavy—citrus cleaner, spent perfume, and something feral. The perfume of freedom.

She sank into one of the shadowed booths, tucked into the crook where two velvet benches kissed. For once, she drank her coffee while it was still hot.

The sun slipped between tall windows, casting long honeyed lines over the worn wood and half-wiped tables. Everything looked different in daylight.

More real. More hers.

Logan arrived like gravity—quiet, certain, coffee in each hand. Hoodie down. Curls wild. Her eyes only for Marina.

She slid into the booth beside her, knees brushing.

"Still working?" Logan teased, nodding to the papers Marina had automatically spread on the table—event lists, invoices, half-read notes.

"Still showing up," Marina replied. The words landed gently.

No bite. Just truth.

Logan nodded and let silence bloom around them.

PART II – INTIMACY IN QUIET

They sat hip to hip. Close. Familiar. A soft buzz of skin to skin through thin cotton and borrowed warmth. Logan's hand draped casually over Marina's knee, fingers curled loosely, like she belonged there. Like she'd always belonged there.

And this time, Marina let her.

No retreat. No shame. No edit.

She leaned into it.

Outside, the city blinked awake. The streetlights clicked off. A cab rolled past, the sound muffled. Inside? Time slowed.

"Now what?" Logan asked, voice still gravel-rough with sleep and sex and something tender.

Marina didn't answer immediately. She stared at the way the sunlight caught in the velvet, turned dust into gold. The sound of the espresso machine rebooting cracked like punctuation.

"I stop lying," she said finally. Her voice was even. "To them. To me."

Logan didn't interrupt.

"I start here," Marina whispered.
Logan pressed her lips to Marina's temple—a kiss that held no heat, just truth. "You already did," she murmured, letting her lips linger.

Marina turned into it, eyes fluttering closed.
She didn't need thunder.
She just needed this.

PART III– THE VELVET BOOTH

But Logan's kiss didn't end at her temple.
It moved.
Slowly. Intentional. With reverence and ache.
Her mouth skimmed along the elegant line of Marina's neck. Marina gasped—soft, startled, aroused.

The coffee mug trembled in her hand. She placed it down quickly before it shattered the moment.

Logan's hand slid higher on Marina's thigh, fingers teasing the hem of the oversized hoodie—the only thing between them.

"You okay?" Logan asked, lips brushing the shell of Marina's ear, her breath warm and wicked.

"Yes," Marina breathed. "Don't stop."

Logan didn't.

The velvet caught Marina's back as she leaned into it, legs spreading instinctively to invite touch, warmth, want. Logan's fingers slipped beneath the hoodie, tracing soft skin, following the path her mouth had started.

Marina tilted her head back, exposing her throat. Logan took the invitation.

She licked. Bit. Sucked softly where the jaw met the neck.

A sharp inhale escaped Marina's lips, followed by a moan she tried to muffle but failed.

"Shh," Logan whispered, smirking, eyes dark and molten. "Someone might walk in."

"Let them," Marina whispered, eyes fluttering closed. "Let them see."

Logan's hand moved higher—possessive, precise. She knew her now. The terrain. The sounds. The places that made Marina gasp, writhe, beg. And she used it.

She slid fingers between Marina's thighs.

Soft cotton parted.

Heat met touch. Marina's rhythm shift—revealed. Her back arched. Hips rose. Fingertips gripped the velvet seat. She chased pleasure like a confession.

Her breath—staggered.

The room filled with the quiet sounds of want: stifled gasps, shifting fabric, the faint hissing of the espresso machine in the background.

The stage was set.

And Logan moved into the space between passion and song.

She kissed her way down—slow, anchored, devout. Her mouth grazed the inside of Marina's thigh, tasting heat and salt and tension. Her hands stroked outward, steadying Marina as she began to shake.

Then—finally—Logan found her.

And when she did, she didn't rush.

Logan let her tongue *cut, cue, cut, cue…*

While she listened for the *drop*.

Every movement was a dialogue: soft, slow, then deeper, deliberate. A language only they spoke, one syllable at a time.

Marina's hands slipped into Logan's hair, not to guide—just to hold on. Logan could feel the intensity behind Marina's grip.

The drop was on deck.

Marina came—hard, quiet. A low, broken sound escaped her lips as her body trembled under the weight of it. No theatrics. No performance. Just a deep release. It rippled through her belly and chest like something sacred had cracked open.

Logan did not move.
She stayed.
Cutting and *cueing* until Marina came again—harder this time.

Logan's mouth pressed against Marina's thigh, breath syncing once again. Holding her like the song wasn't over yet.

Tears blurred Marina's eyes—not from pain, but from everything that had finally released.
Years of hiding, of perfecting, of pretending.
Gone in the space of Logan's hand, her mouth, her love.

PART IV – AFTER

Logan kissed her thigh once more.
Then her navel.
Then her heart.
Then her lips found Marina's lips again—softer this time, slower, like they were rewriting all the mornings they'd never had before.

She pulled back just enough to brush foreheads.
Marina laughed—a shaky, unraveled thing, equal parts joy and disbelief.
Logan pulled the table back and handed her the abandoned coffee mug, which had somehow survived the earthquake of their pleasure.

"Still hot," Logan said, eyes gleaming.
"Not as hot as you," Marina managed, voice low, playful.

They sipped in tandem, legs tangled beneath the table, the velvet sticky against the backs of their thighs. Hair mussed. Lipstick smudged. The kind of beautiful you never pose for.

The kind you earn.

Marina looked around at the space she had built—her altar, her battleground, her rebirth.

Ember & Wax still smelled like yesterday. Still echoed with laughter. Still felt like them.

But for the first time, it felt like hers.

No mask.
No edit.
No compromise.
Just Marina.
Just love.

Logan's foot nudged hers under the table, playful. Anchoring.
Marina smiled.
Small. But unshakable.
The kind that didn't need an audience to matter.

The sun kept rising.
And she didn't flinch from the light.

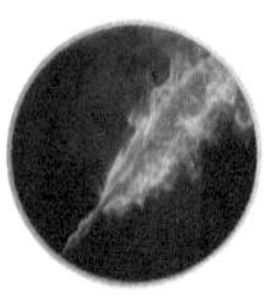

About the Author

Phoenix Cole is a writer from Hockessin, Delaware.

She never set out to be an author — but life, with all its quiet reckonings, had other plans.

Through her stories, Phoenix gives voice to those who live in the in-between — the ones learning to unhide, to love without apology, and to find freedom in their own becoming.

Her work is a tribute to the resilience of the LGBTQ+ community and to anyone who has ever felt unseen, yet chose to keep shining anyway.

Acknowledgments

To those who saw me — even when I was still learning to see myself.

To the friends and chosen family who listened without judgment, who reminded me that love does not need permission to exist.

To the LGBTQ+ community, whose courage continues to shape the world — your stories gave me the strength to tell mine.

To my readers — may this book remind you that you are never alone in the in-between.

And to the ones who believed in this story when it was still just a flicker — thank you for helping me set it free.

Phoenix Cole Press

For the ones who listen between the lines...
this music was made for you.

The lights fade, but the story lingers.

Every note you felt between these pages lives on in sound.

Scan the vinyl below to unlock the *Ember & Wax* playlist —
curated to mirror every heartbeat, hush, and whisper between the
words.

Phoenix Cole · Ember & Wax Soundtrack · Exclusive Edition

The Soft Open is a story of liberation dressed as a love story—raw, queer, and achingly honest.

Marina Clairmond built a life wrapped in velvet and perfection: curated parties, flawless smiles, and silence. But when her meticulously constructed world begins to crack—under the weight of grief, desire, and long-buried truths—she must choose between the role she plays and the woman she truly is.

In the heartbeat of a glittering underground lounge, surrounded by found family, new beginnings, and the pulse of music that remembers what she's forgotten, Marina takes the most dangerous step of all: telling the truth.

And in that truth, she finds Logan Carter—a DJ who sees her without filters, without fear, and loves her not despite her damage, but because of it.

For anyone who's ever lived between silence and song, *The Soft Open* is a fierce, tender, and luminous reminder that the moment we stop hiding is the moment we truly begin.

www.ingramcontent.com/pod-product-compliance
Lightning Source LLC
Chambersburg PA
CBHW020335010826
48970CB00011B/765